Surfer Boy

By
gaël Mustapha

ISLAND HERITAGE

Surfer Boy

Written by gaël Mustapha
Illustrated by Ron Croci

Published by
ISLAND HERITAGE
P U B L I S H I N G
A DIVISION OF THE MADDEN CORPORATION

94-411 Kō'aki Street
Waipahu, Hawai'i 96797
Orders: (800) 468 2800
Information: (808) 564 8800
Fax: (808) 564 8877
www.islandheritage.com

ISBN NO. 089610-302-1
First Edition, Fourth Printing - 2002

Dedication

For my son, Keith Gouveia, who served as inspiration and "surfing advisor" for this tale. And, for my "league of nations-hapa" family including daughters Cathi, Colleen, and Jennifer and Teri Ann and my nine grandchildren and one great granddaughter who continue to provide inspiration for many of Tutu's stories.

About the Author

gaël P. Mustapha, born in Washington, D.C., lived in California as a young child and moved to Hawaii in her early teens. She graduated from Kailua High School with the first graduating class.

After attending the University of Hawaii, she married, had three children, moved to California and earned degrees in journalism and mass communication from San Jose State University. Returning home to Hawaii, she worked for the University of Hawaii, Department of Hawaiian Home Lands, City and County of Honoluu, and the Department of Education; retiring as communications director for the DOE after nearly 20 years of state service.

As a freelancer, she writes travel and personality articles as well as a recipe column for southwestern newspapers. Among her other national and local publishing credits is Kailua: A Community History. Surfer Boy is her first middle-grade fiction work. She has several others in the works.

gaël and her husband, Akema, reside in Green Valley, Arizona. Writing is her passion.

Contents

Illustrations: Page vi, vii, viii, 2, 7, 14, 17, 18, 23, 25, 28, 37, 42, 49, 55, 60, 65, 68, 71, 76, 84, 88, 98, 104.

Surfer Boy

Keoni's mother,
Michelle

Keoni's father,
Jacques

Keoni's Brother,
Micah

Keoni's Brother,
Jeremiah

Keoni's Brother,
Joseph

Cast of Characters

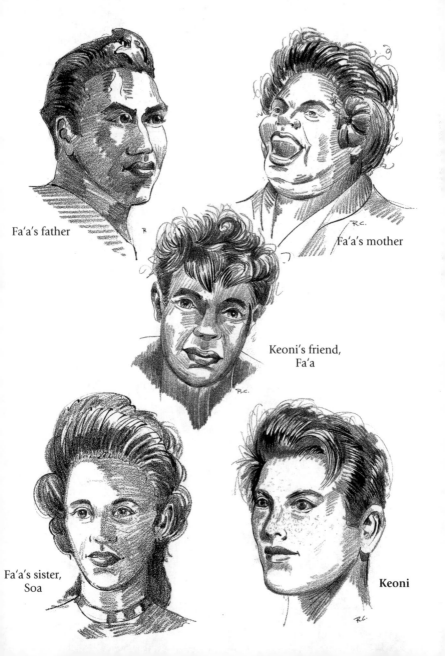

Fa'a's father

Fa'a's mother

Keoni's friend,
Fa'a

Fa'a's sister,
Soa

Keoni

Surf's Up

Keoni grabbed his board, hopped on his bike and took off. He rode around the corner, down the wide palm-lined road in the small town of Laie on O'ahu's North Shore.

The wind blew in his face and the smell of sea spray in the air made him ride faster. Straight down one street, around another corner. He popped a wheelie, almost dropped his board. He skidded into the front yard of his best friend's house.

"Howzit?" Fa'a called, leaning on a rake.

"Come on, man. Surf's up!"

"Wait. I got to finish first." He returned to raking coconut husks into a big pile.

Keoni propped his bike against a tall coconut tree and put his surfboard on the grass. Around the side of the green wood-frame house, he caught sight of Fa'a's family at work out back. Fa'a's jolly

fat mama looked up. She greeted him in Samoan. "*Talofa! Poofaapefea mai oe*, Keoni? Hello," she said in English. "How are you?"

"*Lelei tele*," he responded. "Very well."

She came close, squeezed him to her. The scent of hard work and coconut clung to her as she kissed the top of his head.

She asked, "Your chores all *pau*?"

He grinned, "Surf's up, Mama."

"So." She stood, hands on hips, holding the coconut mid-rib broom against the side of her colorful *mu'umu'u*. "Work first, then surf. Fa'a got to finish up before he go. You wait."

"I know, Mama. I wait." He ducked past her large frame and went to watch Papa and Grampa Talamoa spread the huge *hukilau* nets to dry on the racks.

He called out the Samoan greeting. They responded. "Catch plenty today," Papa grinned. "Fish fry for sure tonight,"Grampa's toothless smile spread across his wrinkled face.

Fa'a's grandmother sat on a *laufala* mat quickly weaving coconut fronds into baskets. Keoni knew they would be used in the village Council House at the Polynesian Cultural Center. Some would be sold in the gift shop there. She was one of the finest Samoan weavers in all of Hawaii.

He stood for a moment, watching Soa, Fa'a's sister as she stooped low in the small dryland taro patch at the back of the yard. He walked close, stooped beside her. Silently, he pulled weeds with her.

Finally, she looked up and smiled. Her smile caused Keoni's heart to beat faster. Her thick dark hair was caught up on top of her head with an ivory comb. Its whiteness shone in the sun against her shiny black hair. Bits of her hair escaped, blew about her face.

Keoni wanted to reach out and tuck those wispy strands in for her. He didn't. Beads of perspiration dotted her dusky skin. "*Talofa*!"

"Come surf with us," Keoni whispered. She stood up. Her cut off jeans revealed long cocoa-colored shapely legs. The faded colorful bandana top she wore barely covered her budding breasts. Keoni inhaled deeply.

"Surf, surf, surf. That's all you ever think of," she said.

"Not really," he grinned. "I think about you a lot too."

"You lucky your father never put you in one all boy boarding school in the middle of the Utah desert," she laughed. The happy sound of her laughter rippled out in waves in the stillness of the late morning.

"Why you say that, Soa?" He lapsed into the familiar broken pidgin English language of the islands.

"You dangerous, 'as why."

"How you mean that, my sweet Samoan

talking chief's daughter?"

"You tease too much. I'm not your anything, surfer boy. Go on, get out of here. Get a job." she stamped her foot. "Get a life. Leave me alone."

"That's no way to treat the guy who will one day be your husband."

"Ha!" She raised her voice. "That will be the day. Get out of here before I yell."

"You'll see," he tossed his head back and laughed. He threw the weeds he held in his hand in her pile and walked back to where Fa'a still raked.

"Your sister sure got a bug in her..."

"Only you, Keoni. You bug her." Fa'a laughed. "You tease and tease. Never know when for stop."

"Only because I like her. All I did was ask her to go surf with us."

"Everybody knows you like her. She scared of your father. He no like for you to like her."

Keoni snarled, "I'm not my father. Let's get out of here."

"I going, Ma," Fa'a said. He put the rake in the tool shed, picked up his board.

Keoni left his bike against the tree. Fa'a didn't have one. They walked down to the main road, crossed the highway and headed toward Pounders at Mālaekahana.

They stopped to watch the sea breaking into foamy crests. The breakers stretched into rolling waves, the joy of all surfers.

Keoni rubbed wax on his board and placed it in the shallow water. He lowered his body onto the board in the waist deep water.

He paddled out toward the breaking surf. Fa'a followed. They pushed on through the swells until they were about 20 yards beyond the break.

Warm water ran in rivulets off their bodies and boards. Their developing muscles rippled in the sun light. Fa'a was the color of dark coffee. Keoni looked more like the finest aged *laufala*. Freckles danced as his nose twitched, catching the scent of an oncoming wave.

"It's going to be a big sucker," he said, kneeling on the long thick balsa-wood and fiberglass board. The wave moved closer.

He caught it, stood up in the side-on position, his feet at a 45-degree angle across the board. He balanced, moving the rear leg and foot slightly. He stabilized his position with his front foot. Balance, judgment, experience, strength and skill took form as he shot forward.

The shoreline moved closer as he flew across the face of the wave. He felt himself flying free, like a bird. Riding a good wave had to be the best thing in the whole world, he thought. Nothing else gave him such a feeling of power, control and total fulfillment.

He kicked out near the beach, dropped to a sitting position on his board. His legs dangled in

the shallow water, nearly touching bottom. He rocked with the tide in white water, waiting for Faʻa.

Overhead, a small plane hummed in the giant blue sky. To his right, the majestic dark green Koʻolau mountain range stood tall and proud.

Small kids romped on the sandy shore. Faʻa paddled up to him. "Too good, you," he said. "I always forget you one goofy-foot."

"Always," Keoni said. "How come you never get that first wave?"

"I wasn't ready." They paddled back out, caught several good long rides but none as good as the first one Keoni caught. The sun dropped slowly behind the Koʻolau range.

"It's getting late," Faʻa said. "I got to head for home."

"One more," Keoni said.

"You, always one more. That's why you always stay in trouble."

"No worry. One more." Keoni paddled out again toward the break. They both rode one more, then paddled into the beach.

At Faʻa's house, Keoni picked up his bike. He called softly, "*Sau se aso*, see you later. Tell Soa I love her," he chuckled.

"Sure thing," Faʻa said. "Hope you no get in trouble. So late already."

Keoni rode into his yard, let his bike fall on the grass. He checked his board for dings.

Carefully, he hosed the board down and then took it around back and placed it to dry in the vertical rack he'd made.

Father stood on the back porch. "John," he said in a voice Keoni knew well. Only Father called him by his English name. Keoni hated it. He closed his ears to the too familiar lecture he'd heard so many times before.

Punishment and Homework

Jacques Lafayette, Keoni's father, an elder in the Mormon Church, taught chemistry at Brigham Young University-Laie Campus. Made of stern cloth, the Frenchman came to Laie in 1969.

From Utah, he brought his petite, meek and gentle wife, Michelle. With them, came their three Utah-born sons, Micah, Jeremiah and Joseph.

They settled into the village of Laie on O'ahu's North Shore without incident. The family arrived only four years after the celebration of a century of Laie's life as a Mormon community.

Like the missionaries that had come a century before, Father had an abiding faith and strength which enabled him to meet life's trials. Keoni learned early in life that he provided one of Father's most difficult trials.

Keoni arrived in the middle of a cold, tropical

winter storm the year after his family moved to Hawaii. He'd been told it was a difficult birth. There could be no more children after Keoni. He'd also heard stories of the family's disappointment at his birth. They had all hoped for a sweet baby girl.

Instead, they got John, called Keoni by the Hawaiian nurse who helped deliver him at the small, 28-bed Kahuku hospital. Family stories claimed Keoni an obstinate, troublesome, different child from the date of his birth.

"Darker than his brothers and such a crybaby," he'd been told. So stubborn, too active, too contrary. "No, no, no," his favorite word from the time he learned to talk.

The family said those things about Keoni. Yet, it seemed to Keoni, they said only good things about his three older brothers.

Micah, so like his father, was a hard worker as well as brilliant. He was a professor of medicine at a California University.

Jeremiah, the follower, upheld the family traditions. He was away on a mission.

Joseph was the youngest student ever admitted to Brigham Young University at Laie. He graduated from Kahuku High School before the age of 16. He had been attending classes at BYU for a year already.

Then, there was Keoni.

"Come in here," Father spoke sharply.

"Yes sir," Keoni said stepping into the pantry

at the back of the house.

His father towered over him. Canned goods lined the shelves. The old man's gray beard and hair made him look like the portraits of the elders of long ago. "What am I to do with you, son? No sense of responsibility. You never obey rules. Do only as you please. You pay no attention to anyone else's feelings."

Father went on and on. "You've upset your mother again. Respect, boy, is an important trait."

Keoni hung his head. He always meant to try harder to live by Father's rules. It was so hard.

He wanted to fly free. Like when he rode the waves. Rules confined him. And, Father had so many of them.

He heard the stern voice say, "Go to your room after you apologize to your mother. You were to have been home over two hours ago. Late again." The voice droned. "Your surfing privileges are revoked for the next two weeks. Do you hear? Two weeks."

"I hear," Keoni said. To himself, he added, "You really know how to hurt a guy."

His father added one more insult. "You will not get your driver's license for at least two more months. If you can't keep commitments about time, how can we trust you with the car?"

Keoni quickly apologized to his mother. He wondered if he'd be allowed to eat supper as he went to his room. Surfing made him super hungry.

Father hadn't even raised his voice. The cold, quiet tone demanded obedience. Keoni wanted to punch a wall. White hot anger boiled in his stomach.

Anger at Father and at himself for being late. For being grounded and for another delay in getting his license. At the rate things seemed to be going, he'd be an old man before he got his license.

He knelt beside the bed and pounded his pillow. The joy and excitement of riding waves dimmed to a memory. He brooded.

They expected too much of him, he decided. He wasn't brilliant like Micah or docile and obedient like Jeremiah. And, he certainly wasn't like Joseph. He didn't even want to be like any of them.

He didn't know just who or what he wanted to be. But not like them.

He wished he was part of Fa'a's family. Fa'a got in trouble sometimes, too, but that was different. The love in his friend's family seemed real. You could see it, feel it. His own family seemed so cold, uptight. They cared only about Church, proper behavior, education and proper behavior.

Keoni hated being a *haole* professor's son. He tried to stop thinking about it.

He picked up his guitar and began to play. He picked at the strings, tuned up and played softly

the music in his head. A sorrowful, haunting melody that had come to him one day last week. He'd meant to write it down in his notebook. Later, he'd add it to the growing pile of tunes that stuffed the black notebook on his desk.

He fiddled with chords, loud, discordant sounds. He thought of Soa.

His anger began to melt away. How beautiful she is, he thought.

He imagined her practicing the *taualuga*, the final dance in a special program. Tall, proud and graceful, he could see her with the vibrant ceremonial headdress perched on top of her head. He leaned back, closed his eyes...she danced only for him in his daydream. He'd seen her dance for others a few times at the Center.

Finally, he opened his eyes, retuned the guitar and played two slack key numbers that Soa's grandfather had taught him. He liked the calm feelings that always spread through him when he played the guitar.

Thoughts of Soa excited him. These two things made him feel almost as good as flying free on a perfect wave.

"Keoni," his mother called, interrupting his day dreams. "Supper."

"Be there in a sec," he answered. His stomach grumbled with hunger pains. He stood the guitar in the corner, put on a shirt and raced to the table.

Father asked, "Can't you ever walk? Did you

wash?"

Keoni hurried into the bathroom, washed his face and hands. He ran a comb quickly through his tangled hair. The list of rules never ends, he thought, listing dinner rules in his head.

"Wear a shirt. Wash. Wait until Father sits to be seated. Elbows off the table. Don't reach across the table. Ask for things to be passed. Chew with your mouth closed." It was enough to make you lose your appetite.

Good thing Mom was a great cook. The food cooled while Father said one of his endless blessings.

Keoni knew when he grew up and had a family, the blessings would all be short and fast. Or maybe I won't even allow a blessing at all, he thought. I'll be making the rules then. He didn't hear Father say "Amen" and continued to stand.

"Sit down, Keoni," Mother said. She ladeled bowls of a hearty beef stew and passed them around the table. Father picked up his spoon, sampled it and nodded approval. At last, they could all eat when they had finished passing the rest of the food around.

Keoni loved the homemade bread with lots of butter and guava jam. They also had a salad of carrots and raisins. He ate two servings of stew. He thought about a third. Instead, he ate two pieces of deep-dish apple pie.

After supper, he returned to his room to do

homework. He struggled with a paper on Laie's history for his Hawaiian studies class.

He wrote, "Laie is the educational, spiritual and cultural center of the Mormon Church in the Pacific. A phenomenal transformation took place in our community since the first missionaries came here.

"Laie, a small primitive village about 40 miles from Honolulu, was considered a 'City of Refuge' in ancient times. That meant any person in trouble could be safe from all harm if that person could reach the sanctuary of Laie.

"King Kamehameha II abolished that system. But later, Laie once again became a sanctuary for people when the Mormon missionaries came in 1865.

"What started as a barren, treeless plain with only a few crude *pili* grass huts and small taro patches grew into what you see today. Lots of houses, trees, flowers, wide streets and people of many nationalities working, playing and worshiping side by side. And, of course, the Temple, Brigham Young University, which had been called Church College of Hawaii...and the Polynesian Cultural Center, called PCC."

Keoni stopped to read what he had written. He decided Mrs. Faaumu, his teacher, would know he copied some stuff from the library reference materials. He didn't usually use words like "phenomenal transformation" and "sanctuary."

She'd know. He had to find other words. The dictionary was in Father's study. He didn't want to go in there. He couldn't think of any other words.

He set the paper aside. He had wanted to write about the history of surfing. Mrs. Faaumu had told him, "Keoni, I think it will help you more and our class, too, if you write about our community's history. You are a good writer. I will be sharing the better papers with the class."

She added, "Besides, Nolan already talked to me about his paper. It's on surfing."

Keoni had to hand the paper in the following week. Since he couldn't go surfing, he figured he'd be able to finish it on time.

Lucky for him, Laie celebrated its 100th anniversary under Mormon ownership in 1965. The librarian, Mrs. Miyamoto, helped him find old newspaper clippings and a whole memory book about the community. Otherwise, he would have been lost because not very much had been written about Laie.

Mrs. Faaumu suggested he talk with some of the old timers. "I'm sure they could tell you about long ago days in Laie. Some of the retired plantation workers and the elders of the Church would probably like to talk story with you."

Keoni didn't think he wanted to do that. He had read most the stuff he borrowed from the library. He might talk with Fa'a's grandfather. He'd been in Laie a long time.

Keoni circled the copied words so he would remember to change them and then he stuck the paper in a folder. He worked five algebra problems easily and then piled the books on a chair near his guitar.

He took off his shirt, threw it in the corner and flopped on his bed. He laid on his back and stared at the ceiling. His thoughts wandered back to the beach. He dreamed of riding the waves. Someday he would have his driver's license and could go further up the coast to surf the big ones. At Waimea, Banzai Pipeline, Sunset and maybe even at Mākaha.

Someday, he'd be good enough to enter surf meets. He scratched his head and dreamed of bringing home trophies. He'd pile them up for Soa.

She fascinated him. Her tawny skin, thick black hair and full lips that invited kissing. When he could drive, he'd take her for a ride. Maybe she'd let him kiss her. His skin tingled. He felt a stirring.

His thoughts and his body's reaction to thinking about her troubled and excited him. He knew about sex. Some of the guys at school talked about it a lot. Some even said they had done it. Some bragged about doing it often.

The teacher who showed the sex education movies said the guys who talked most about scores often are only just talk. Keoni didn't talk about it and he hadn't done it yet. But he thought he wanted to.

Sometimes he felt like an animal lived inside him waiting to get out. That scared him. There wasn't really anybody he could talk about these things with. Father would freak out. Keoni doubted that Joseph or even his other brothers ever even thought about sex.

He reached down, touched himself. He looked around the dark room to make sure no one saw him. It felt good. The quickening hardness sent a sense of power through him.

Thoughts of Father's stern face and the church's teachings made him limp. Sweat formed on his forehead. He got up, put his shirt back on. He sat on the bed and pulled on his sneakers. He tied the frayed laces.

He slipped unnoticed out the back door. He ran around the corner, down wide palm-lined Hale La'a Boulevard away from the Temple. He cut through Moana Street and ran faster in the direction of the Polynesian Cultural Center. The Center had closed and was dark.

His heart beat fast. Still, he ran, trying to shake the mixed up feelings roiling inside like angry winter waves. He circled in the Center parking lot and headed back. This time, he ran down Iosepa Road and all the way to Fa'a's house.

He slowed down as he approached the house. He jogged in place near the coconut tree where he'd propped his surfboard earlier in the day.

Lights shone out of the dark house. Soa crossed in front of her bedroom window. Her silhouette behind the thin curtain filled the window for less than a minute. The light went out. He wondered if she had climbed into bed or gone out of the room.

He slumped against the coconut tree, holding his side. Sweat ran down his chest and under his arms.

A half-moon peaked out from behind the clouds. Dark palm fronds rustled in the tradewinds like giant sky sweepers. Soft night sounds filled the air. A dog barked. Cats howled. Something stirred in a bush near the tree. Keoni caught sight of the dark figure of a small mongoose scurrying across the road.

Car lights rounded the corner. Keoni flattened himself against the tree. He didn't want to be caught slinking about Soa's house. That would mean more trouble with Father for sure.

The car's engine raced as the old Ford Mustang sped by. Keoni caught sight of the teenage boys who filled the front and back seats. The car careened round the corner.

Keoni knew Father would call them "juvenile delinquents. "After the car had gone, Keoni jammed his hands deep into his surfer shorts pockets and hurried away into the night.

He walked fast around the corner back down Hale La'a Street. He headed straight to the front

of the Mormon Temple. So big it stood, like a giant, towering over the sleeping village. The fountains, pools, tropical foliage and the vast grounds were imposing. Keoni knew this giant on the hill was, according to Father, a citadel, a site for nourishing learning, wisdom and moral strength.

Keoni peered into the night at the giant. He wondered why he did not or could not seem to catch those things from this place, the gathering place of church members. He found no comfort or solace here. He felt lost and alone.

He turned away and went back down Hale La'a once more, crossed the highway and hurried to the beach. The night surf pounded in his ears. Small white caps shone in the moon-lit sky.

The wind struck his face, caused him to shiver. He stood listening, silent and small against the giant ocean, so much bigger than the Temple. A sense of peace began to spread through him. This was his temple, his place for feeling whole and at one with nature.

He wished he could explain the feelings the ocean gave him to Father. He would never understand. Maybe, *I can explain it to Soa someday. I think I could make her understand*, he thought.

Finally, he turned away. He walked home slowly and crept quietly into the house. He stood in the hot shower a long time, letting the water needles sting his skin. Finally, he fell into bed and slept.

Talk Story

The next week sped by. Keoni decided to go talk story with Soa's grandfather before he finished his paper.

"*Talofa!*" Keoni greeted Grampa Talamoa one afternoon after school.

"Come, sit boy," the old man beckoned to him. Keoni sat on an old coconut stump. He watched the old man's gnarled fingers fly as he repaired a *hukilau* net.

His hair, the color of steel wool, curled tightly about his head. The deep wrinkles in his face traveled every which way like a road map. Dark eyes flashed. His toothless grin invited talk. "How you do in school, boy? You stay smart like Joseph? Hoo, that boy be something else."

Keoni waved his hand. "I'm not like him."

"If you go try..."

Keoni shook his head. "But I'm working on a paper for class about Laie's history. I know you been here a long time."

"That's right," Grampa Talamoa nodded his head. "Shish, I forget how long already. I think the first Samoans came Hawaii about the time of World War I. Maybe 1919, something like that.

"About the time they go build the Temple. Was not too long after that when my family come. Maybe 1925 when get maybe 30, 35 Samoans living Laie already."

He grinned. "Shish, when I first come here, me small kid, you know. I never know quite why we came this place. Come by horse da kine. Pali stay only dirt path those days. Had to put straw bags like shoes on the horses' feet so they no slip." He stared out toward the sea, a far away look in his eyes. Keoni knew he was sliding across time to those gone-by days.

"You know the Mormons stay Lana'i first. Then come here after da kine troubles. I forget just what." He said, "Still had sheep, cattle, goats and plenty horses when I come. More country than now."

He grinned. "Had the sugar cane, too. You know that cane the thirstiest buggah in the whole world? To make one pound sugar, you need 4,000 pound water. Can you believe that?" He scratched his head. "Water stay big problem for Laie those days. For long time 'til they make those wells."

He frowned. "Sometimes, those guys who come more early than me had to eat *'ape*, fern roots and the fish they go catch. Only food they get. Hard times in Laie, you know."

He stretched his legs. Keoni leaned his head on his hands and listened as the old man continued to talk. "Things better when us guys come. My father worked plantation. Make 25 cents for work one whole day. Can you believe that?"

He scratched his head again. "And not even real money. They call it Laie script. He use it at the village store for buy da kine. Spam, flour, cornbeef, li'dat. We never had that kine in Samoa. So, real treat. "He told of one brother working at the dairy. Another took care of the mules.

He told, too, about the way things went up and down in the village. "Before World War II, had really hard times. Plenty people move away. Not much work for do. Then war time come, 1941 that time. Pearl Harbor, you know. You go read about that in your history, I'm sure. When Japan bomb us."

"Plenty work for the war effort. The house all fill up again. After war, come slow again. Up, down, up, down, that's how this place all the time."

He added, "Then they make the college. Things get better again for all us. This is good for young people from all kine places in the Pacific... Tongans, Fijians, Tahitians, more Samoans, the

Maori. The young ones come for go school."

He said, "Course you know then they start Polynesian Culture Center. PCC they call 'em, the villages for each da kine. Each group can hang on to its culture. Get jobs. Get jobs for the students. The visitors come. They like see us natives."

Grampa laughed. "But good too for them to see our arts, crafts, hear our language, li'dat. Good for us, too. We learn from each other."

He wiped a hand across his forehead. "Shish, I been talk plenty. I nevah talk so much for long time already. Must be my, what you call that? Heritage. My family been talking chiefs, you know. "He smiled. "But of course, you know that already."

Keoni smiled. The old man laughed some more and then went on again. "Even though we adjust, learn American kine ways, I guess we stay Samoans at heart. We nevah go leave the old ways behind of us. Like Soa's gramma go say, we must gotta stay strong and brave. Keep the traditions alive for the young ones coming up."

He set the net he'd been working on at his side. "You know, just like how her *laufala* stuffs, da kine weaving. She always make sure she go, you call that interweaving the good parts of America and the good parts of Samoa and the good parts of Hawaii for make one better weaving."

He closed his eyes. "Nuff already, boy. I stay tired. Talk too much."

Keoni said softly, "*Faafetai*, thank you. You gave me so much to think about." He added, "If I get a good grade on this paper, be because of you."

Grampa waved him away. "I just tell 'em, you get for write 'em. That's hard. I no can. See boy, you stay more smart than me."

Keoni shook his head. "But you wise, Grampa." He touched the old man's shoulder as he rose to go in a gesture of thanks. Keoni went home. He sat in his room for a long time, thinking about all that Grampa Talamoa told him. Finally, he began to write.

When he finished his paper a few days later, he asked Joseph to type it for him. His older brother finished typing it the following day.

When he returned it, he told Keoni, "This is good. I bet you get a good grade on it."

Keoni smiled. "Thanks," he said.

"I like the part where you tell about old man Talamoa and the interweaving of the best parts of many cultures. Comparing it to the old woman's baskets." Joseph laughed and pushed his dirty-blond hair out of his eyes. "You're quite the storyteller, little brother. Maybe you'll become a historian or a writer one day."

"Fat chance," Keoni said. "I couldn't have written it without reading the stuff or without talking to Grampa Talamoa. He's the one who made it come alive and interesting." He added,"And I wasn't even going to talk with him."

"Don't put your abilities down all the time. You don't have to go through school as fast as me to be smart, you know. "Joseph stretched his long frame out on the extra bed in Keoni's room.

"In this family, you got the toughest row to hoe. Following along behind Micah, Jeremiah and me. It's not easy. I know that."

"Father doesn't."

"He does," Joseph said. "He just forgets sometimes. Don't let him make you feel dumb. You're not."

Keoni said, "I sure feel that way a lot."

"Think about the Polynesians you wrote about--the Samoans, Tongans, Tahitians and all the rest. Look at their art--weaving, carving. Each one is different from the other. Some are finer, some more primitive. That doesn't make any one the best or smartest. Each is special."

He went on, "Just like us. We're all different. I'm not like Jeremiah or Micah. I'm me and that's okay. They got their strengths and talents. I got mine. So do you. Use yours to become what you want to be."

Keoni laughed. "I should talk to you more often. You make a guy feel like he's worth something. But how am I going to ever please Father when all I like to do is surf and play music?"

Joseph laughed. He sat up. "That's a hard one, little brother. I'm not sure. You'll figure it out in time. Besides,"he said, "What's important is to please yourself, to feel good inside you."

He tapped Keoni on the chest with his finger. "Be patient. It'll happen. You'll find your own way. In time."

"I hope so," Keoni frowned as his brother walked out of his room.

On The Waves Again

Keoni got an "A" on his paper. Mrs. Faaumu read it to the class. They all clapped. Keoni felt embarrassed. Good feelings spread through him.

At home, Father did a very rare thing. He praised Keoni's paper at the dinner table. Joseph winked at him. Mother beamed. Father said, "I knew you had it in you. You just have to put your mind to it, nose to the grindstone." He added, "As a reward, your surfing privileges are restored three days early."

Keoni clapped and yelled, "Right on." "No need for such a loud display of emotion," Father said.

Keoni settled down, not wanting to blow what he'd just earned back. Father nodded approval and said, "This Friday, I have no classes. I will take you down to Kaneohe to get your driver's license. Hopefully, you can pass the test. Mother will send a note to the school requesting your release."

Keoni was beside himself. He had to sit on his hands and bite his tongue to keep from hollering his joy.

Right after supper, he asked for permission to go surf. "I'll be home before dark. I promise."

He hopped on his bike, balanced his surfboard and sped to Fa'a's house. He'd been tempted to go alone. Safety and the buddy system, he knew as keys to not getting in trouble in the water. Besides, if Father found out he surfed alone, he might never get his driver's license.

He dropped his bike, stood his board against the coconut tree and hurried to the open front door at his friend's house. The Talamoas were just finishing dinner. He started to retreat to the porch to wait.

Mama and Grampa motioned Keoni inside. Samoan greetings exchanged, Mama invited him to sit down and join them. He did. They asked how he was. He told them everything in a rush. Grampa nodded with pleasure over the good grade. Fa'a clapped him on the back. Soa smiled.

"So, I want to catch a couple waves before dark. To celebrate. Can you come, Fa'a?"

"I wish I could," his friend said. "I promised Grampa I'd go with him for deliver a *hukilau* net to his friend in Kahalu'u."

Grampa said, "Go, boy. It can wait."

Mama said, "No, it can't. You promised."

Papa nodded. "Grampa get one sore back. Hard for lift up the heavy net."

Keoni's face fell. Soa looked at her mother. Mama nodded. "I'll go with you, Keoni," Soa said.

Gramma said, "Go now, Soa. I'll clean up for you."

Soa hurried out of the room. Keoni smiled his gratitude and offered to help clear the table while he waited for Soa to change.

Keoni could not believe his good luck this day. A good grade, on the waves again and a chance to be alone with Soa. She came back into the room. She wore an old *puka* T-shirt over a Samoan-print bikini. "Let's go," she said. "I can borrow your board, Fa'a?"

He nodded. "No ding 'em."

"I'll look out for her," Keoni promised.

Outside as they hurried up the road, Soa said, "I'll look out for me, thank you."

"Soa, you know what I meant. We look out for each other." He relaxed, felt comfortable walking beside her. She'd gone to the beach many times with Keoni and Fa'a or with others. But this was the first time for just the two of them.

"Thanks for coming, Soa," Keoni said shyly. "I need to feel the wind in my face, the *'ehu kai* on my back and hit the waves again."

"The ocean is your friend, right?"

Keoni answered, "You got it." He added, "You my friend, too, you know."

"I know that, Keoni. Sometimes you scare me, you know."

"I don't mean to." They had reached the beach. "Sit with me for a minute." He sat down on the coarse sand. She hesitated. "Watch the sets," he told her. She dropped onto the sand near him, stretched out her long tawny legs.

He watched the waves. She looked around. The sun had just slipped behind the mountains. They sat, silhouetted against the pink and crimson sky.

The waves were mushy, not very big. "We don't have much time," Soa said.

"I know. Let's go." They moved into the water. They paddled silently side by side around the oncoming waves out to the line. No one else was in the water.

They sat on their boards, watching. "Here it comes," Keoni said. "Catch this one," he yelled moving into position in an easy fluid motion. His front foot pointed forward, the back one at a right angle as he crouched with his knees bent. The board tail lifted up the face. He shifted his weight to the rhythm of the swell. He danced along the wave in a style perfected by Gerry Lopez at Pipeline years before.

He caught sight of Soa off to his side slashing and tearing in the more radical and aggressive style of the '80's. He admired her strength and ability.

They both kicked out at nearly the same time. They turned and paddled back out. She smiled across the water. "A good one."

"For both of us. Go again." They rode another one. Keoni faced the longer wall, twisted his knee and pushed his foot down to step on the gas. He flew faster, imitating Soa's style this time.

He felt free, alive. A sense of power surged through him.

The sky darkened. "One last ride," he called to Soa. She gave him a thumbs up sign.

The tide changed. It started to rise. The swells had grown larger. He decided to show off, do a 'hang ten', an old popular surf move.

He stabilized his board, walked to the nose, wiggled all ten toes over the edge. He looked to see if Soa watched. She did.

He waved, lost his balance and wiped out. So much for his fancy style and form, he thought, swimming to the surface. He swam after his board, then paddled to shore. Soa stood on the beach, waiting.

She laughed. "Show off," she teased. "I know. Good fun, though."

She said, "We better get a move on so you no get trouble."

"Right," he agreed. "I'm glad you came," he said, taking hold of her free hand.

He smiled at her, relaxed. "Know what I like

best about surfing?" She shook her head.

"The total freedom. No rules. No boundaries. The testof each wave. Every single one is different." He hurried on. "You can be creative, use your imagination to deal with each wave. Try something new, different. No one says, 'You gotta do it this way' or 'this is the only way'." She nodded, squeezed his hand.

He squeezed back. "Soa," he said softly and then stopped, not sure of what to say next.

"You better go," she said as they walked into her yard. Mama called from the doorway. "Come, come inside, both of you."

"Not tonight," Keoni said. "I got to get home before dark. I promised."

Mama waved her hand in the air. "Never you mind. I called you house already. Spoke with your father. He say okay for you to have *puligi* with us."

Keoni yelled, "Hot dog." He loved Mama's special steamed coconut pudding.

"Not 'hot dog,'" Soa laughed, whopping his arm. "*Puligi, puligi.*"

After they'd eaten the sweet, tasty pudding, Soa took a medium-sized *laufala* sitting mat from the pile near the door. "Come," she said. "Too hot inside. Let's sit out back under the coconut tree."

Mama smiled at Keoni as he followed Soa out the door. He heard Mama say, "I think those two stay sweet on each other."

Papa laughed. "Remind you of the days when

I stay sweet on you?" The rest of their words were lost to Keoni and Soa as she moved deeper into the shadows of the yard. She spread the mat beneath the coconut tree farthest from the back door.

"Are they right, Soa?"

"About what?"

"That we sweet on each other?"

"Maybe," she said, her eyes downcast. Her white teeth shone in the dark as she smiled. The tradewinds whispered softly in the palm fronds above them. Soa had not put her T-shirt back on. Keoni watched the rise and fall of her breasts as she breathed.

He took both her hands in his. He pulled her gently into his arms. She did not resist. He kissed her eyes, then her lips. She tasted of salt water and coconut pudding.

She put her hands on his bare chest and then pushed him away. "You scaring me," her voice sounded husky.

"Why?"

"You know, Keoni. I'm afraid I like you too much."

"Why? What do you mean?"

"You belong to Professor Lafayette. We so different. You *haole*, me Samoan."

"So? I'm not my father, you know. I'm me." Keoni raised his voice, "Get that through your thick head. I don't care about him or what he thinks."

"But we so young," Soa said. "I never liked a boy before."

Keoni laughed. "I never liked a girl before either." He shook her gently. "In Samoa, you be old maid already." "Laie not Samoa." She sighed. "I'm so mix up inside."

"Me, too. About plenty things. But not about you. I want you to be my girl." He felt surprised at how easy it had been to say those words. He had wanted to say them for a long time.

She looked away but let him take her into his arms again. This time, he put his arms all the way around her so she couldn't pull away easily. She leaned against him.

Her skin felt so soft. A fine salt spray felt powdery on her back beneath his fingers. They stood together for a long moment.

Gently, he pulled her down on the mat with him. She didn't stop him. He kissed the tip of her nose and then her lips again. They kissed hungrily.

He felt a warmth and a rise in his shorts. Embarassed, he released her.

She stretched out gracefully like a cat on the mat on her stomach. She crossed her arms beneath her face.

He sat beside her, stroked her thick damp and tangled hair. He ran his finger across her cheek and touched her lips.

She nipped him playfully. "Be careful. I bite," she teased. He ran his hand across her bare back and then stretched out beside her.

She turned over and moved into the cradle of his arms. In silence, they watched silver-gray clouds scudding through the shadows of the moonlight through the coconut trees.

Keoni whispered, "I wish this day would never end. It must be the best day of my whole life." Soa rolled up on one elbow. She touched his lips, his face and ran her hand across his chest.

"You getting hairs." She pulled one of three fine threads growing there. He moved her hand, embarassed again. She leaned over and kissed him full on the mouth. He held her tight against him.

The back porch light went on. He quickly released her and sat up. He shivered. She giggled.

"Now who's scared?" "I just don't want your Mama to say I can't be with you any more."

"No worry," Soa laughed. "They know. You heard them."

"But..."

"I'm a good girl," she said. "They trust me."

"They might not trust me and maybe they shouldn't," Keoni's voice sounded husky.

"I'll keep you in line, Keoni."

"You may have to," he said seriously.

"No worry," she laughed. She jumped up, pulled the mat out from under him. "You better go now. Before your father gets mad."

He rose, pulled her to her feet and held her close. "You my girl?"

She nodded. He kissed the tip of her nose. They walked around to the front of the house.

Gramma and Papa and Mama sat on the front porch. Keoni waved farewell and thanked Mama for the *puligi*.

He waved and walked home with a spring in his step and his hands jammed deep in his pockets. His heart pounded in his chest.

It wasn't until he was in the shower that he remembered he'd left his bike and his board at Soa's. He hoped Soa or Fa'a remembered to put them around back. He didn't want to call so late. He hadn't even hosed down his board.

Having a special girl could make you forget things.

Phone Calls

After school the next day, Keoni went to Soa's to get his bike and board. Both were gone.

He asked Fa'a, "Didn't you put 'em in back when you came home?"

Fa'a said, "I never saw 'em. Remember, you left late."

Keoni asked Soa, "You didn't see them either?"

Soa looked at him with a dreamy expression. "I went to bed right after you left." She whispered, "I wanted to remember and dream about everything you said."

Keoni smiled at her. Then, a look of despair crossed his face. "But my bike and my board. That was a custom-made Lightning Bolt. I saved so long to get it. All those hours I swept classrooms to earn the money for it." He kicked the coconut tree they stood under.

Fa'a said, "Maybe someone just borrow 'em."

"Sure," he said.

"Well," Fa'a said hopefully, "You know how some of the newer Samoan kids are around here. Those who just came from Samoa. They not raised like us. They see, they take. Not really take," he amended. "They borrow, then bring back."

Keoni ignored him. "Geez, my father will do his whole number about how irresponsible I am."

Soa said, "Let's go talk to Papa. Maybe as talking chief, he can find out something."

Fa'a frowned at her. "You know he doesn't like to go along with all the old ways now."

"Mama will make him," she said. "He can talk with other leaders in the community. Maybe find out something. Grampa will help, too."

"We can try," Keoni said. "And let's go walk around, go to the beach. Maybe we'll spot them."

They talked with Papa Talamoa. He made a few phone calls. He didn't find any answers.

The three of them scoured the neighborhood, went to the beach. Keoni scanned the line, watched carefully as the surfers came in one by one. No sign of his bike or board.

He knew it was almost supper time. He had to go home soon. He hoped Father wouldn't notice. For sure the dream of getting his license would burst like a soap bubble. Fighting anger and tears, he told his friends good night.

"You know I'll call you if we find out anything," Soa squeezed his hand. "I'm really sorry."

He walked home slowly. He felt more concerned about the board than the bike. The old bike had been handed down from Jeremiah to Joseph and finally, to Keoni. He could live without the bike, especially if he got his driver's license.

But his board was his key to freedom. He'd never get another like it. Jobs were scarce, especially if you're only 15. The school had given his old job cleaning classrooms to Nolan. The head janitor told him, "Nolan's money will help his family. You got parents who take care you. Nolan's dad stay out of work."

Keoni understood. He didn't like the job anyway. It had cut deeply into his surfing time. But he liked the money. Father didn't believe in allowances. He believed you had to earn your own way in this world.

He didn't believe in paying for home chores either. As a family member, you had certain responsibilities and were expected to carry them out.

Taking out the trash, cleaning yard, keeping your room neat, making your bed...all those things were more of Father's rigid rules.

Keoni didn't say a word at supper. He picked at the food on his plate even though meatloaf and baked potatoes with bacon and melted cheese on top were just about his most favorite foods. No one noticed his sullen silence. They were all too busy talking about some special community event to be held in the spring.

Father said, "It's an event to increase the spirit of Laie. It will express our gratitude for those of Polynesia who have stood firm in the faith against trials and tribulations. It will also pay tribute to the continuation of Mormon ideals and Polynesian culture." Father droned on and on.

"That sounds marvelous Dear," Keoni's mother said. "Any way I can help..."

Keoni finished dinner and finally asked to be excused from the table. He carried his plate to the kitchen. He scraped the meat into the cat's bowl on the back porch and threw more than half his potato in the wet garbage container. He used his fork and mooshed it under other wet garbage so nobody would see. He didn't need a lecture on wastefulness.

He went to his room and picked up his guitar. He played the same mournful, haunting tune he'd composed a couple weeks ago. He'd forgotten all about it until he started plucking chords.

He found an empty music sheet and wrote down the notes. He ran through it again and again, changing certain notes on the paper.

Joseph passed his half-open door. "What a dreadful dirge. Enough already. Play something happier."

Keoni ignored his brother's remarks. He continued to perfect the piece of music. Finally, he had it the way he wanted.

But there was no sense of accomplishment. He thought of yesterday. He'd been so happy and high, on top of the world. Like being on a perfect wave, shooting the tube at Pipeline. Today felt like a total wipe out, as if he'd been scraped and bruised on the finger coral bottom. His temples throbbed. His stomach ached. He turned the light out and flopped on his bed.

He didn't hear the phone ring. Joseph called him loudly, "Keoni, you deaf or what? Answer the phone."

Soa's voice sounded breathless. "Keoni, come quick. It's just like Fa'a said. You know who's Salanoa?"

Keoni could hardly understand a thing she said, "Slowdown. You're talking so fast."

"You know that new kid over on Naupaka Street? The one just came from Samoa for stay with his grandmother?" She added, "He's younger than us."

"What about him?"

"He borrowed your bike and your board. He brought 'em back. They stay here now. He told Fa'a thanks for the use."

"Geeze," Keoni said. "I like bus' his head. The nerve of that guy."

Soa laughed. "You *haole*, you really don't understand. He didn't steal 'em. Only use for a while."

"But he didn't ask or tell. He just took what didn't belong to him."

"Never mind. Come now."

Keoni hung up. He told Father he'd forgotten his board and bike at Fa'a's. "I'm going to get them."

"A little young to be getting absent minded," Father said. "Don't stay late. You must get up early so we can get to Kaneohe when the police station opens. If you're not there early, you may not get to take the road test." He smiled, "I'll let you drive down. You can use the practice. Make sure you don't forget your permit."

Keoni waited patiently for Father to finish. When he did, Keoni took off like a shot.

He checked his board carefully for dings and other damage. The skeg seemed a bit loose. He kept quiet about it, just glad to have it back. He knew he could fix it.

Soa said Papa had talked with Salanoa and his family. "He explained that in Hawaii what Salanoa did is considered stealing. I don't think he'll do it again."

"I just got to be more careful," Keoni said. "Thanks for getting it back." He hopped on his bike, moved closer to Soa. "I can't stay tonight, even though I want to. Driver's test tomorrow morning, early." He stole a quick kiss from her.

She pinched his shoulder. "You a stealer too," she laughed. "You no ask or tell. Just take. Thief," she stuck her tongue out at him.

"That's different," he protested. "You my girl."

"Same, same," she teased. "Go quickly now and good luck on your license. Do good."

"I'll try," he said and rode away into the night.

Keoni didn't hear the second phone call later that night. But as soon as he entered the kitchen in the morning, he knew something was radically wrong.

Tears streamed down his mother's cheeks. Father looked grim. A deep worry line furrowed Father's forehead.

Keoni asked, "What's wrong?"

His mother wept. She dabbed at her eyes with a dish towel. Father frowned. "Get hold of yourself, Michelle. This outburst won't help matters."

Keoni asked again, "What's wrong?"

Father answered, "There's been an accident."

"What kind? Who?"

"Be quiet, son. Let me finish. It's Jeremiah."

"What happened?" Keoni felt icy fingers of fear race along his spine. "Is he alive?"

Mother sobbed. Father said, "I'm trying to tell you if you'd quit interrupting."

Keoni looked at the bowls of cold oatmeal on the table.

His usual early morning appetite disappeared. He waited for Father to go on.

"From what we know, he was riding his bike, making missionary calls. The car didn't see him.

"Oh, no." Keoni sucked in his breath and groaned. "How bad?"

"We're not sure. The hospital said he's holding his own. Your mother will fly up tonight. That's the earliest I could get a flight for her. I'll go tomorrow morning. We'll bring him back here as soon as he's able to travel."

Keoni fought mixed feelings. That meant no driver's license today. Concern for his brother won out. "What can I do to help?"

"Be a good boy while we're gone," his mother said quietly. "Mind Joseph. He'll be in charge."

Father said, "Micah has flown up already to consult with the other doctors. That's all we know. There are some broken bones but we don't know how extensive the damage is."

Mother sobbed. "Why can't we go now? Why is Hawaii so far from everything? Why don't the planes fly more often? Why Jeremiah? He's such a good boy. No trouble to anyone."

"Michelle," Father said, gathering her small frame in his arms. "Calm yourself. Don't take on so. He'll be all right. I just know it."

Keoni felt sad and happy at the same time. Sad about his brother but happy to see Father try to comfort his mother. She seemed so tiny and helpless against his big frame. Like a little old rag doll.

He'd never seen Father hold or kiss his mother before. Father seemed more human in that moment.

Keoni sensed their need to be alone together. He got up from the table. "I'll get ready for school," he said.

"Wait, son. If you're up to it, we'll go ahead and go for your driver's license. There's nothing else we can do here until it's time to take your mother to the airport."

"Nothing," his mother said in a small voice, "except to pack, make sure the freezer's stocked for the boys and worry. The not knowing is so hard," she sobbed again.

"Michelle," Father said, "Joseph will be here with you. Both boys know how to cook. I have complete faith in them. Church members will probably invite them in to eat anyway. And, it won't take you more than an hour to pack."

He went on, "Who knows when I'll be free to take Keoni again? Best we be done with it. We'll be back in time to get you to the airport. Keep busy while I'm gone. Idle hands," he said in a commanding tone.

Mother nodded, "You're right of course,

Dear. I didn't mean to fall apart." She dried her eyes, scraped the untouched oatmeal into the garbage container and put the dishes to soak.

"You should eat something before you go, Keoni," she said. "Shall I make you some toast to eat on the way?"

"I'm not hungry, Mother." "All right, Son," she said, pulling him close, kissing his cheek. "All my boys," she sighed. The tears started again. "Good luck with your test."

"Let's go, Keoni. Are you ready?" Father asked. Keoni nodded.

"Keep busy, Michelle," Father added. "We'll be back as soon as we can."

The Road Test

Keoni drove carefully from Laie to Kaneohe. The long drive down Kam Highway wandered through many small towns. Hau'ula, past Kahana Bay, Crouching Lion, Ka'a'awa, Kualoa Beach Park, Kahalu'u and finally, into Kaneohe.

The gray sky threatened rain all the way. The humid, sticky weather caused perspiration to run down under Keoni's arms. He kept his eyes on the road.

In the beginning, Father talked about driving. "Don't ride the clutch, shift. Not so fast. I should have had you practice stopping on hills a few more times. Your parking experiences are minimal." he sighed.

Keoni kept silent, concentrating on the road. He hoped he'd remember all the traffic safety laws. He worried about failing the road test. Father

made him nervous. He willed himself to stay calm. He concentrated on what he had to remember.

Father next talked about the weather. "Winter is upon us. Nearly time for the big surf. I know, to you, that means surf meets. Which one is first?"

"I think it's the Smirnoff," Keoni answered. "Because of the controversies the last few years, it's hard to keep them all straight. I watch the newspapers and listen to the guys to know what's going on. There's the Duke and the Masters at the Pipe. I want to go to that one for sure."

"Hard to believe that the sport of Kings has gone from pure recreation to an international activity and a giant industry," Father said. "Boards, clothes, magazines, TV specials, movies." He shook his head in disbelief. "A whole way of life. I hope you don't have any great ambitions of becoming a surf bum."

Keoni didn't respond. He pulled around to the back of the Kaneohe Police Station. He found a spot and parked next to the library. Father opened the door.

"Here's the no-fault insurance card. You'll need it. Have you got your learner's permit?"

"Right here," Keoni tapped his back pocket. They entered the examination room. About four people stood in line ahead of him.

"Don't be nervous," Father said. "I'll wait for you in the library. Come get me when you are through. Good luck."

Keoni stood outside awaiting his turn for the road test. He tried to relax.

"Lafayette," the older Japanese man called.

"Here," Keoni raised his hand and moved forward. Disappointment welled in him. He had hoped for the Hawaiian guy. His friends had told him the Japanese guy didn't like *haoles*. Most of his friends who had the Japanese guy had to take the road test more than once before getting their licenses.

Keoni led the examiner to the car. He showed him the no-fault card.

The man said, "Step on the brakes, boy. Okay, your tail lights work. Your safety inspection is current."

He got in the car. "Ready, boy? You buckled up?" Keoni nodded. The clipboard on the examiner's lap looked awesome. "When you get to the top of the hill, make a right turn."

Keoni started the car and got up the police station hill with ease. He put his blinker on for the turn, eased the clutch out and didn't turn too wide. He reminded himself he'd been driving with Father in the car for the past year without any real problems. The examiner couldn't be tougher to drive with than Father.

He paid careful attention to the instructions, stopped before the crosswalk line and made sure to drive within the speed limit. Before he knew it, they were turning the corner back into the police station parking area. Keoni parallel parked between two cars without any trouble.

"You're a good driver," the Japanese man said. "Stay that way. Don't hot rod, speed or drive recklessly. You'll live longer."

Keoni sighed with relief. He thanked the man, went inside, put his toes up to the line the woman showed him, had his picture taken and was finger printed. He wiped hard at the black gunk on his thumbs. He paid the fee.

It was over. Keoni was now officially a licensed driver. A proud smile filled his face. His friends had been wrong. The Japanese man had passed him on the first try. He walked into the library to find Father.

Father looked up from the newspaper he read. "Congratulations, Son."

"How'd you know?"

Father laughed. "Your smile says it all." He winked. "Besides, you have the paper right there in your hand." Keoni grinned.

"Let's get a move on. I'll drive home. Your mother is waiting for us. I wish I could have gotten on the same flight with her. I worry about her."

"I hope Jeremiah is all right," Keoni said.

Father sighed, "So do I. So do I." He pulled out onto the highway and headed home.

On the long ride back to Laie, they started talking about surfing again. Father said, "I tried it once. I couldn't get the hang of it. That was when we first moved to Hawaii." He went on, "I'm not an athletic man. Never have been. Didn't have time for recreation."

He continued. "You think I'm a hard man. You should have seen my father. No time for play or idleness. Work, work, work and study. He was determined we would all be properly educated."

Keoni looked at Father in a new way. He had never really heard Father talk about his childhood. Keoni smiled. He couldn't imagine Father in a pair of shorts let alone on a surfboard.

Keoni felt a certain kinship with Father for the first time as they hurried down Kam Highway. Outside the car window, he watched the raw, untapped energy of the Pacific swells. All along the coast, an angry sea pounded the shore. *'Ehu kai* or sea spray almost as thick as rain drove a misty fog inland across the road. Keoni liked the sound of the Hawaiian name for the spray.

The angry sea stirred excitement inside Keoni. North Shore winter storms meant big surf. Now, with his license, Keoni wondered how soon he'd get guts enough to do more than watch at Waimea and the Pipe.

Tons of water crashing down a mountainous wave could collapse and crush boards and bodies. Rips snaking toward the open sea could carry inexperienced surfers off course to watery graves. Still, the jaws of the Pipe beckoned.

Every surfer flirts with danger, death and

destruction. Man pitted against the elements.

Keoni sensed a primal urge to test his will against those odds. Even the few surf meets he'd gone to had a feeling and sense of a primitive carnival.

Sun, sky, sand, sea, man and woman too. He thought of surfing giants from Hawaii's past... Duke Kahanamoku, Lopez, Lynn Boyer, so many others. At the Pipe, it all comes together on nature's watery turf to test strength, will and endurance.

This year, Keoni would be a part of all that. Excitement roiled deep inside him. He opened his mouth. The words tumbled out.

"Father, does the ocean excite you?" Without waiting for an answer, he rushed on. "Me too. Each wave so unpredictable, no two alike. Every surfer responds to the rise and fall of a swell in a different way. You challenge a giant wall of water with sheer guts. Oh sure, skill, determination, ability and will, too. Everything plays a part but it's a very personal thing."

Keoni couldn't stop talking. "You have to put it all together. Balance, strength, courage, skill. There are no boundaries or rigid rules. If you do it right, you fly free. Ride with the wind. There's nothing like it. The feeling, the high. It's raw power," he finished softly. His voice held awe and respect for the great sea. "The alternative is a wipe out."

Father looked at him. "I'm not sure I understand all that you've said. But I understand your feeling and your intensity. My faith gives me the kind of feeling you describe." They rode in silence for awhile, each enveloped in his own thoughts.

Finally, Father said, "That's what helps sustain me. Why I know Jeremiah will be all right. I must believe."

Keoni nodded, hoping Father's faith would hold true. Father parked the car in the yard. They went inside.

Mother's bags stood near the door. She sat in a rocking chair holding a wet cloth to her eyes. Joseph sat quietly reading on a sofa across the room.

They talked briefly about Keoni's driver's license and last minute instructions. Then, Father said, "We have a little time before we must leave. Let's pray together as a family for Jeremiah." A frown crossed Father's face. "My extra class load has kept us from our family prayers too often."

They knelt together, held hands. For once, Keoni did not resent the ritual of family prayer.

Father led them. When they'd finished, they stood. Mother kissed Joseph and Keoni. "Take care, my sons. Pray often for Jeremiah's full and speedy recovery and our safe journey."

"We will," they said.

The Big Surf

After Joseph returned from taking Father to the airport, Keoni asked to use the car. Joseph said he could.

He picked up Faʻa, Soa and Nolan. "Surf report said eight to ten at the Pipe. Let's check it out."

They attached Nolan's racks to Father's car, stowed the boards and took off.

Lots of cars crawled along Kam Highway with boards on top heading in the same direction. Radios blared.

Tourists parked, watched the shoreline with binoculars and snapped photos of western swells against a stormy sky. Rain showers moved slowly inland.

Surfing's main arena stretched along 15 miles of sand and lava rock on Oahu's North Shore.

Favorite spots were already crowded with parked cars, shave-ice and manapua wagons. Hawaii's youth, out in force, gathered to watch sets, brave the breakers, face the long green wave peaks, cresting, collapsing with crushing force.

Keoni found a place to park. Nolan took his board. The others decided to leave theirs and watch sets first.

"No sense taking them if the waves too big." They walked to a spot near the center of 'Ehukai Beach Park, site of the famed Banzai Pipeline.

They stood for awhile and watched. Strong surfers crowded the line-up. White water churned outside the reef. They knew that meant the waves could be up to 15 feet. Cameras with bazooka lenses on tripods dotted the sand, trained out toward the sea.

A broken board flew through the air. "Geez," Keoni said.

"Look at him go." A powerfully built surfer dropped from behind the peak, driving under the cascading lip into the tube. He disappeared behind the silver curtain. For what seemed like forever, he was out of sight.

Then, he shot into view, rode with the wind before kicking out. "Wow," Nolan said. "Did you see that?" He grinned. "Check that radical guy over there."

Two surfers collided, resulting in a horrendous wipe out for both. Boards flew. Keoni

watched as one surfer threw his hands over his head to prevent being hit on the head by the flying board near him.

Soa sat down on the sand. "You guys go if you like. I'm not getting myself killed today. Too big."

Keoni reluctantly agreed with her. He wanted to go, to impress her. But he knew he was out of his element. He was not experienced enough to handle surf this big. Disappointment bubbled up in him. He didn't want them to think him chicken.

They had all agreed on the way down. If the waves were too big, they wouldn't surf. It was tough to bring the boards and then decide not to go.

Fa'a said, "I not going either. Too big, man."

Nolan said, "Your choice. If you guys like be wimps and panties, ok by me. But I going." He was in the same grade as Fa'a and Keoni but was two years older and bigger. He stood several inches taller than Keoni. He lifted weights, had a well developed chest and arms.

He had surfed Pipeline quite a few times over the past couple years. He usually hung around with the juniors and seniors because of his age. Also, some of them had wheels.

"Good luck," Fa'a told him.

"Be careful," Soa added.

They watched him paddle out to join the lineup around the incoming waves. They lost sight of him in the crowd.

Nolan took off on a wave. He didn't adjust his weight fast enough. The tail lifted up too far.

"There he is," Soa yelled. "He's not going to make it." The nose of his board went too deep, ending in a classic pearl dive and a bad wipe out.

Nolan wiped out more often than he rode but he hung in there and kept trying. After a while, Soa and Keoni walked up to the road. He bought rainbow flavor shave ice for them. They sucked up the sweet, cold syrup mixture through the tiny straws and nibbled at the ice.

"Ono," Soa said. Keoni kissed her cool lips.

"You, too," he winked at her.

They found Fa'a talking with some other guys who had decided not to surf. "Crazy, man. Too big."

"I no like crack my head." The surf-stoked group talked and watched as the sun moved across the sky toward the west.

Nolan finally came in. Tired, he sunk onto the sand. "It's big," he said. "You guys more smart than me." He panted. "Summer waves made me lazy for big surf. I'm out of condition."

"You got some good rides," Soa said. Fa'a and Keoni nodded.

"I wish I had your nerve," Keoni said.

"Got to get in better shape," Nolan said. "Better run and swim a lot more before you try 'em." After a while, they piled into the car and headed home. Soa invited Keoni to have supper at her house. "Mama said it's okay. Tell Joseph to come, too."

Keoni dropped Nolan off, went home, showered, dressed and talked Joseph into going with him to the Talamoa's. They walked over.

The family gathered in a circle at prayer. Soa read from the Samoan Bible. Mama motioned Keoni and Joseph inside. They sat down quietly on the *laufala* mat. Mama whispered, "You know, this is one of the ways we keep our native language alive. We be through soon."

Soa's voice rang true and clear in the musical language of Samoa as she finished reading the passage. Then, Gramma led the family in song. Neither Joseph nor Keoni knew enough of the language to sing the words. They did know the tune and hummed along.

The harmony of Grampa and Papa's deep rich voices with Mama and Soa's soft sweet sopranos and Gramma's alto blended like a full-on church choir.

"Beautiful," Keoni said. "I feel I should clap but I know better."

"Dinner stay simple tonight," Mama apologized. "Nothing fancy. *Palu sami.*"

Soa said, "You had it before. Coconut milk, taro leaves, onion and salt."

"Fresh fish, too," Grampa beamed. "Good catch again."

"Baked in coconut cream, the fish," Gramma smiled. "We glad you join us. Hard for you with your mother and father both gone." She spoke for all of them. "We include Jeremiah in our prayers. We hope he be okay."

"We hope so, too," Joseph said. "Father will probably call us tomorrow to tell us more."

"Be sure you folks let us know," Mama said, "if anything we can do for help."

After supper, Soa cleared the table and washed up the dishes. Keoni and Joseph talked with Grampa and Papa and Fa'a. Gramma sat in another part of the room weaving baskets while Mama strung shell *leis*.

When Soa finished cleaning, she stood in the doorway, caught Keoni's eye. She signaled him to come. Keoni slipped away and they walked to the beach. They held hands.

"Your family is so relaxed, Soa. Everybody does their work and seems happy. Nobody gets tense or uptight. I feel so happy at your house."

He paused. "My house is so different. So formal. So...*haole*."

Soa laughed. "My house not always calm either, you know. When Papa get mad, watch out. He hit first, talk later. That's Samoan way."

"But at least if you get lickin', you know what it's for. Then it's *pau*, over. You forget and go on."

"Not so easy as that. It hurts when I get lickin'"

"How long since you get the last one?"

"Long time now but I'm growing up. When the older boys, my bigger brothers and my other sister stay home, was hard. We all get plenty lickin' but since they went America and Tulu to Maui with her husband, stay easier now. Of course, everybody put up a squawk when they first go. But we all use to them being gone now. But our house not so calm in those days."

She added, "And when you get lickin' you don't even deserve, you no forget so fast. Things just stay better now."

"Probably was hard when you folks had so many living home because cost so much money."

Soa sighed, "Could be. Fa'a and I learned from the others, too. We don't make trouble. I'm a good girl, remember?"

He pulled her against him. "I know. I respect you for that." He kissed her. They walked along the water's edge carrying their rubber slippers. Wet sand squished between their toes.

"Do you ever think about leaving Laie some day? Like your other brothers and sister?"

"Not really," Soa answered. "Laie is my home. Always has been. I'll probably get married, have kids, just like Mama. Stay right in our same house forever. Samoan tradition."

"But do you ever think about more than that? College? Your brothers and sister went away."

"If I go college, I'll probably go BYU, work PCC. I know Mrs. Faaumu says we should all go away for a while, try new things, see the world before we make up our minds." She giggled. "I guess I could join the service." Keoni laughed. "You? No way."

"Why not me?" Soa's voice took on a sharp tone. "Girls can join, too, you know. Lots of Samoans been in the service. How you think most of them came Hawaii in the first place?"

"I know that, silly goose," he said. "But you don't seem the type."

"And just what's your idea of 'type'?"

"Well..."

"Well, nothing," she scoffed. "Listen surfer boy, girls can do almost anything these days. Mrs. Faaumu said."

Keoni tried to change the subject. "You want to take a ride with me tomorrow? Maybe we'll go to Waikiki after church."

"You changed the subject, Keoni. I not through. Maybe I will go college and move to California and become, a... oh heck," she laughed. "I don't know what will happen to me in the future. I just live day by day. And yes," she added, "I like go Waikiki tomorrow. I'll have to ask Mama."

She danced down the beach ahead of him. "I haven't been to Waikiki for a hundred years."

"You're not that old, girl," he said, chasing her. He caught her, pulled her down on the sand. They kissed. Finally, she pulled away.

"You're scaring me again." She turned around, sat against him, staring out to sea. "So what will you do with your future, Keoni?" She asked softly, "What you like be when you grow up?"

He held her close. Lifted her heavy hair and kissed the back of her neck. "I wish I knew. It's so hard to decided. I like surfing. I think I'd like to compete around the world, make money like that. Others did it." He sighed. "But I gotta be realistic. I'll probably never be that good."

"You gotta believe in yourself."

"Father would never approve anyway."

"So?"

He sighed again. "I like my music, too. I wrote lots of songs, you know."

"Sing me one," she said.

"I don't have my guitar. Next time I come over, I'll bring it."

She clapped her hands. "Good, you can play with Papa and Grampa. We can all sing. I love to sing." She giggled. "Maybe I'll become a torch singer in Las Vegas or in the movies. Not many Samoans in show business." She giggled again. "You can be my manager and guitar player."

"That a good one," Keoni laughed. "Keo-Soa. That could be our name."

"Oh you," she stood up. "Soa-Keo sounds better. Ladies first." She took his hand and pulled him to his feet. "We better go home now or I might get the first lickin' I had in a long time."

They walked home slowly hand in hand. "Do you ever think about going to Samoa?"

"Once in a while," Soa answered. "It might be nice to see where my family came from. Trace my roots," she said.

"Tell you what," Keoni chuckled. "After we're married, we'll go to Samoa to trace yours, and to Utah to trace mine."

"Sure, surfer boy, tell me another fish story."

"I mean it, Soa. Not now, tonight or tomorrow or next week, but in the future. You wait and see."

Jeremiah Comes Home

The next morning, Father called. Joseph answered the phone. Father told him, "We hope to be home by the end of the week. His condition is improving. He has a broken leg, a broken arm, scrapes and bruises, contusions and 27 stitches in his head. They have to run more tests. But he's alive and mending."

Joseph assured Father that everything was fine at home. "Give Mother our love and prayers. Jeremiah, too. We'll see you when you return. Let me know the flight schedule. I'll meet you at the airport."

Father said, "Ask Elder Meisen if you can borrow his station wagon. Put the back seat down so we can make Jeremiah as comfortable as possible. We'll be in touch."

Later Joseph explained to Keoni. "I'm not

sure Father would approve of you driving to Waikiki but..."

"I'll be careful. I promise."

Keoni picked Soa up after church. They drove to Kaneohe and up through the Wilson Tunnel. Down through Kalihi Valley and onto the H-1 freeway. They took the Punahou cut-off, turned onto King Street, and then right onto McCully.

They passed Waikiki Gateway Park on Kūhiō Avenue, found a parking place and locked up the car. Then they walked down to Kalākaua Avenue. The mile long strip is one of the most famous in the world. Waikiki Beach is right in the very heart of Hawaii's visitor industry.

People come from all over the world to play and vacation at this famous beach. Soa looked around wide-eyed.

So many people! So many *haoles*, too. Fat tourist men in plaid shorts and loud colorful aloha shirts that didn't match.

Soa giggled. "Look," she pointed. "I thought you only see them in movies. Sometimes, too, at PCC."

Keoni teased. "It's not nice to point. No act like one *kuaʻāina*."

"But I am a country girl. You know that." She held his hand tight. "Don't let go. I'm afraid of getting lost in this crazy cement jungle."

They took a side street down to the new Halekulani Hotel and then over through the grounds of the old pink Royal Hawaiian Hotel dwarfed by all the high rise hotels. They watched limousines pull up in the circle drive and deposit visitors at the first hotel built in Waikiki when it was hardly more than a swamp.

"I guess you gotta be rich for stay here," she said.

Keoni nodded. "Let's go to the beach," he said.

They cut through the hotel grounds to the beach. Wall-to-wall bodies of all sizes, shapes and colors covered the sand like beached sea creatures. Umbrellas shaded some.

Others flopped on large towels. Many sat against striped canvas beach chairs. Sunglasses made black holes in faces. White sun screen covered noses. Gorgeous tans and terrible sunburns sat side by side.

Thousands of heads bobbed in the water. Wind surfers and sail boats dotted the horizon. Surfers formed a line beyond the breakers.

"It's like a giant carnival," Soa squealed. They walked along the beach as far as the old Moana Hotel and then cut back up to Kalākaua. They strolled through the busy International Market Place.

Small stalls displayed shells, beads, jewelry, clothes, food, almost anything you could think of. The beehive of activity gave Soa a headache.

Keoni bought paper cups of fruit punch.

They sipped them as they walked around. "Let's get out of here," Soa said. "Too many people."

Keoni agreed. "Let's go to the zoo," he said. They did.

It was quieter there. They watched the monkeys, the long-necked giraffes and the lions pacing in their cages. Soa shivered in the reptile cage. "I don't like creepy, crawly things. I'm glad they're behind glass at least."

After they walked all around the zoo, they went outside where artists had paintings hanging on the fence. They looked at water colors, oils and batiks of clowns, island scenes and flowers.

"Let's go home, Keoni. I'm tired." They walked to the car and headed home. They rode as far as the Pali tunnel in silence. As they came out of the second tunnel, Soa sighed loudly.

"Oh, Keoni, I'm so glad to be back on this side of the island. Town is too busy. Too fast and too many people. How can people stand it?"

She took in the cerulean blue water, the breath-taking sweep of the Windward coast. "I am a *kua'āina*. A real country girl at heart. I'm glad you took me today, but I don't want to go Waikiki very soon again."

Keoni touched her cheek. "You're funny."

"I bet the mainland is worse. San Francisco, Los Angeles and New York. I'd be scared to death," she said.

"Don't worry, I won't be taking you to any

of those places real soon."

"I hope Jeremiah's okay."

"I do, too." Keoni said, "When someone in your family gets sick or something, you feel so helpless."

"I know," she said. "Pray about it."

The following Sunday, before church, Father called. "Our plane will arrive at 10:00 tonight. Did Elder Meisen say you could use the station wagon?"

"It's all set," Joseph told him. "We'll see you tonight. Have a safe journey."

Keoni decided not to go to the airport. "There will be more room for Jeremiah and all the bags if I stay home." Joseph agreed.

Keoni straightened up the front room, took out the trash and made sure all the dishes were washed, dried and put away. He called Soa. They talked on the phone for a long time.

Not long after they hung up, the doorbell rang. The sight of Soa on the front steps surprised him. "We just hung up," he smiled at her.

"I can't stay since nobody stay home but you. Mama told me for bring these." She handed him a large foil-wrapped loaf of warm banana bread and two large sprays of orchids.

"I'll help you fix the flowers for the table. Put the banana bread in the pantry or ice box and find me a vase."

Keoni couldn't find his mother's vases. Soa went into the kitchen, checked several cupboards and finally found one. She filled it with water, fixed the flowers with *palapalai*, a fern, in a pretty arrangement. She carried them to the dining room table and placed them in the center of it. She stepped back to admire her handiwork.

"Beautiful," Keoni said coming up behind her. "Mother will be surprised and pleased." He wrapped his arms around her.

She leaned against him. "You're beautiful, too," he whispered in her ear. "I wish you would stay."

"It won't look right," she said pulling away as the doorbell rang again. Soa answered the door and greeted Elder Meisen's wife who stepped inside carrying a large pot of stew.

Soa took it into the kitchen. Mrs. Meisen followed her. "We should put it in the ice box. I thought it would be nice in case anyone is hungry when they get home from the airport or for tomorrow night's supper."

"Thank you," Keoni said. "I know Mother will appreciate your kindness."

"My Mama sent the flowers and banana bread," Soa said. "I just brought them over. I have to go now." She waved to Keoni and hurried out the door. Mrs. Meisen stayed just long enough to welcome two more church women coming up the walk. One brought a large fruit salad and the other handed Keoni two loaves of home-made wheat bread.

Keoni thanked them both. After he put everything away, he sat in the front room. The silence in the house seemed loud in his ears. He flipped on the TV.

A lonely feeling swept through him. He hoped his family came home soon to fill the house. He looked at the clock. It was after ten. They should have landed.

Keoni napped but started up when he heard the car in the driveway. He opened the door and ran outside.

Father lifted his hand in greeting. "Come, give us a hand." Mother looked tired and haggard. Dark circles rimmed her eyes. Keoni kissed her.

Keoni stared at Jeremiah. His older brother motioned him closer, grabbed Keoni's hand with his good one. "I won't break," he grinned.

"You already did that," Keoni laughed, lightening the mood.

"You're right. Just like Humpty Dumpty, I had a great fall," Jeremiah said easily. "Fortunately for me, all the hospital doctors and nurses put me back together again."

"And with prayers, love and care, we'll make you whole again, Dear." Mother smoothed back the sandy-brown hair on his forehead.

"First things first," practical Joseph said. "We got to figure how to get him from here to the house."

For the first few days, everyone treated

Jeremiah like an invalid. They all tiptoed past his door, keeping very quiet. He slept a lot since he was tired and weak. Within a few days, he began to gain more strength.

His left arm and right leg were broken, making it almost impossible to use crutches. One of the church ladies brought over a wheel chair which he could manage. The yellow-purple bruises under his eyes faded. Mother bought dry shampoo and washed his hair for him, being careful around the spot where the 27 stitches had been. His hair had begun to grow back where they had shaved his head.

Slowly, he improved. Keoni spent a lot of time with his brother. They talked about his mission, school and the family.

Jeremiah said, "There were plenty of times when I felt angry and resentful at Father, too. When I was your age," he said, "I wanted to be a cartoonist. You probably don't remember."

"You always did draw good," Keoni said.

"True, but Father said, 'And how will you support a family? How many cartoonists make a living wage in this country?'"

Jeremiah laughed. "When I was even younger, I wanted to be a clown." Keoni made a face. "Seriously, little brother."

He went on. "I saw one at the circus and thought I'd be good at it. I love to make people laugh. Maybe," he sighed, "Because we don't laugh enough in this house. Never have."

He wheeled his chair over to the chest of drawers in his room. He leaned over and pulled open the bottom drawer with his good hand. "Aha, look, I found them. See," he held up a box containing tubes of theatrical grease paint. He smiled. "I used to lock my door and shut myself up for hours. I'd paint myself with different clown faces."

Keoni laughed. "I can't believe it. And, I can't believe you still have the stuff."

"Want to try them?" They spent the next hour making themselves up as clowns. "Good thing I broke my left arm or I'd never be able to do this," Jeremiah said.

He'd left his bedroom door open. Father passed by, stopped, came back. "My stars," he gasped. "What's going on here? Are you off to a circus?" Jeremiah laughed. "We're having a little fun. I was telling Keoni about my clown ambitions."

Father asked with a straight face, "Does that mean you still intend to pursue that line of work?"

"Of course," Jeremiah said. He teased, "Didn't I tell you I've been offered a spot at Florida's Disney World?"

"Are you serious?"

"Of course," Jeremiah laughed. "It's honest work."

Father frowned. "But your education, your

mission..."

"Come off it, Dad. I'm just having some fun with Keoni. Relax. You know my mission was almost over anyway. When I'm back on my feet, I intend to go back to school, get a master's degree." He added, "I'll probably end up teaching right here at BYU just like you." He added, "But not chemistry, clown make-up instead."

Father sighed. "You always were the clown in the family."

A smile played at the corners of his mouth. "Okay, boys. Have your fun."

After he'd gone down the hall, Jeremiah said, "You just have to learn to humor the old man. He's a good person right to the core. He just gives the appearance of being a stuffy, uptight, crusty old Mormon chemistry prof."

Keoni said, "You know how to deal with him. I don't. He's so critical. Even now, he jumped to conclusions and..."

"Just give yourself time. You'll learn, and remember," Jeremiah said, "He's more critical of himself than of anyone else." He changed the subject. "Soa's really grown up in the year I've been gone. She's gorgeous," he winked.

"I know," Keoni grinned. "I think I'm in love with her."

Jeremiah chuckled. "Slow down, boy. You got years ahead of you for love."

"But..."

"No buts. Take your time. Go easy."

"She's a good girl and has very proper moral standards as Dad would say."

"I'm sure of that," Jeremiah said. "But the flesh is weak. Remember the teachings."

"How can I forget?"

"It's easy under the right-or should I say wrong-circumstances."

"Wait and see," Keoni said. "I intend to go to college. I really think I'd like to study music. Composition, theory, all that. But someday, I will marry Soa. She's special."

Jeremiah grinned, "Nothing wrong with that. Careers in music are not that easy to come by. Good music teachers are always needed. But, Keoni," he cautioned, "Don't make your plans in cement. You may change your mind a hundred times before you're grown up. That's okay, too."

He added, "Enjoy life. Enjoy being the age you are now. Don't tie yourself down to anything just yet. Life is too short."

He said seriously, "I learned that when I thought I was going to die. It was a very frightening experience." He added, "I very quickly learned to be grateful for each precious day."

Keoni nodded. "I guess we ought to take this stuff off before dinner." He laughed. "I don't think Mother wants two clowns at the dinner table." Jeremiah laughed. "She might be able to handle, but you can imagine Father's face with two clowns at family prayers."

Banzai Pipeline

Keoni listened to the surf report every day. Winter generated fairly steady high surf. He and Fa'a went to watch some of the competition trials at Pipeline.

Two surfers in the trials found out just how treacherous the dangerous breaks could be. One was rushed to Queen's Medical Center with serious head injuries. The other broke a leg. Newspaper accounts said their power cords had saved their lives.

A veteran surf pro was quoted in the newspaper. "If you surf here regularly, it's not a question of if you get hurt but when? These tremendous waves break in very shallow water. Less than six feet deep. Sometimes, you're moving about 30 to 40 miles per hour. That's fast and can be very dangerous."

The danger fascinated Keoni. He heard that two surfers withdrew from the competition after the accidents. "Too big," they claimed. They knew their limitations.

"No shame in that," Keoni said. He added, "I'm going to do it."

"What?" Fa'a laughed, "You going enter the competition?"

"No. But it's only breaking four to six today. Let's go. You game?"

"We go," Fa'a said. "Just because we go doesn't mean we have to surf."

"True. But I got this feeling inside me. I got to do it. To get ride of the fear." "If you think about that, you done for." Fa'a jerked his thumbs up. "Just go for it."

"Nolan said he thinks about the good rides he had in the past when he goes out. The thrill and satisfaction of those rides are what fill up his mind while he's paddling out to the lineup. Otherwise, he couldn't do it either."

When they arrived at the famous Pipe, Fa'a said, "Wow, not so crowded today. Smaller waves 'as why."

They didn't stop to think. They took the boards off the racks and carried them into the water after waxing them.

They joined several others in the line-up. Waiting and watching. Keoni felt the power of the water walls surge beneath him. He knew the jaws of finger coral lay below.

He concentrated on watching the waves and remembered the thrill of an especially good ride at Pounders. He knew he could hold his breath a long time and that he could swim long distances under water.

He'd surfed full on for more than two hours plenty of times. He was in good condition. He knew somehow today was the day. He had to conquer Pipeline or it would conquer him.

He saw the big mother moving toward him. No time to think. Move it out.

He dropped from behind the peak, moved forward, adjusted his stance to keep his balance. He raced the cascading lip, turned just in time to stall and pull into the tube.

A perfect tube. A perfect ride. The ultimate Pipeline ride. He exhaled the breath he'd sucked in. His left hand felt the water. The silver curtain.

He felt at one with he sea, zipping along in the fashion of the kings of years gone by. Today's boards were lighter and smaller than the long boards used by those ancient men.

The thrill of conquering nature remained unchanged. What a feeling. What a high.

Keoni rode it out, savoring every second. After what seemed like forever, he kicked out.

Fa'a came up beside him, wide-eyed. They signaled thumbs up and smiled at one another.

"Hot dog," Keoni yelled. "I did it. We did it.

Go again."

Their confidence soared as they conquered wave after wave. "Not so different from Pounders after all." Keoni let out a yell. "I can't believe it."

Fa'a agreed. "But not so big as usual. We got to remember that."

"I know," Keoni said. "But it's a start. A few more and we better go, too. The sun's starting down."

Keoni misjudged the next wave, moved too fast. He got sucked over the falls, drilled. He felt coral scrape his stomach. He couldn't find the surface. He stayed down. He knew his lungs would bust soon.

Cockiness and over-confidence had taken hold. Made him careless. Pride, too. These things flashed through his head. He wondered if he would die here at the Pipe. It happened to other surfers here. He wouldn't be the first.

Refusing to let panic take over, he struggled upward.

At last, his head bobbed above the water. He sputtered, gasped, taking in great gulps of fresh air.

He located his board and swam for it. Now he was sorry he'd forgotten his cord.

He knew he had to ride again right now. He couldn't let the knot of fear in his stomach grow and overtake him.

Fa'a paddled alongside him. "You okay?"

Keoni nodded, pointed toward the break.

"One more." Fa'a nodded. He understood.

Keoni rode again. No wipe out. It wasn't the best of rides but he did it. He paddled for shore.

Out of the water, he checked his stomach. Three pink pricks and a scrape just above his belly button. He wiped at the blood dribbles.

My badges of courage, he thought. He'd wear them proudly for a few days. He felt grateful they weren't worse.

Fa'a looked at Keoni's belly. "They won't even leave scars. You lucky."

"I know it," Keoni agreed. They slapped hands. "We did it! We did it! Surfed Banzai Pipeline."

On the ride home, they were quiet. Surf stoked. Exhausted, pride of accomplishment, and the triumph over fear and the jaws of the Pipe surged through them. Keoni dropped Fa'a at his house. He leaned out of the car window. Soa came up and congratulated him. They talked for only a few minutes. The light in her eyes shone brightly. Keoni knew she wanted to share his triumph.

Strangely, he wanted to be alone for a while first. He wanted to savor his feelings and the thrill himself. He didn't want to share just now, not even with Soa.

He kissed her cheek and said he'd call her later. "I don't want to be late. Don't want to lose my surfing privileges again," he winked at her.

At home, he hosed down the board, put it in

the rack. Inside, he hurried to his room, not ready to talk with anybody. He stood in the warm shower for a long time. He relived every minute of the afternoon. Finally, he turned the water off, stepped out of the shower, toweled himself dry and slipped into a pair of clean shorts.

In his room, he flopped on the bed, still savoring the high of having surfed at Pipe Line. Next will be Makaha he thought. He picked up his guitar and strummed the instrument. He played softly until Mother called him for dinner.

Family Togetherness

Keoni and Faʻa surfed Pipeline a number of times during the winter season. Almost always, when it wasn't too big. They joined the crowds to watch the competitions.

Keoni dreamed of the day when he would be good enough to compete. Soa went with them sometimes. She was busy practicing for the special Polynesian Cultural Center program. Keoni didn't see her too often. Their activities seemed to take them in different directions.

Jeremiah's injuries healed rapidly. He got the cast off his arm and finally, off his leg. After his college classes, Joseph took him to physical therapy to help strengthen his muscles and speed the recovery process.

Keoni looked forward to the long Christmas recess from school. There would be more time for surfing.

The Christmas holidays promised special times. Good things to eat. Lots to do. Special church pageants and the concert at PCC.

Even Father seemed to relax a little bit during this special season. Keoni thought it might be because Father had vacation, too. He didn't have to work so hard during the holidays.

Mother enjoyed the busy season and all the preparations. She seemed happiest tending to her family when she had lots of people to cook for.

Even the smells in the air added warmth and a goodness to the season. Special spiced cinnamon scents made the house smell good. Mother baked pumpkin and persimmon breads. She also made pies and stored them in the freezer to share as gifts with neighbors and church members.

This year would be extra special because Micah was flying home from California. The whole family would be together for the first time since Micah went away to medical school years ago.

One evening, everyone sat in the living room after prayer service. Mother remarked, as she always did at this time of year, "This is the season when I miss living on the mainland." She went on, "I remember the years when grandparents, cousins, aunts and uncles gathered to celebrate the holidays. Such a sharing you boys don't know anything about or can't even imagine."

A smile filled her face. "The cold, ice skating

on a frozen pond." She hurried on, "Ooh, the wooly mittens to warm the hands and colorful woolen caps to keep our ears warm."

"I don't miss the snow," Jeremiah said. Keoni couldn't imagine living where snow fell and made everything cold all the time. No surfing. Of course, they enjoyed skiing and sledding there. But all those clothes that people had to put on to keep warm!

Keoni preferred Hawaii. He didn't think he'd ever live on the mainland.

Another night, Mother brought steaming mugs of hot cocoa and cranberry bread on a tray into the living room. She smiled. "This is my favorite time of day," she sighed. "Everybody's home safe and well fed. Our prayers are done. It's time for relaxing, sharing with loved ones. Family. That's what life is really all about."

Father frowned. "Michelle, you always worry too much about our safety."

Joseph said, "It's well that she does, Father. Look what happened to Jeremiah. Mother may look like a tiny little mouse. And most of the time she's the quiet one of all of us, but she is the strength and the heart of our family."

"That's as it should be," Father said.

Jeremiah said, "That's not always how things work out in families today. Divorces do happen." Father frowned. "Mothers drink, fathers beat their children. Lots of mothers have to work, especially in Hawaii. There are so many homeless. Those are the realities that some families have to face every day."

"Not in our family," Father said sharply.

"Because you won't permit it, Father?" He hurried on. "I met families on my mission that were in great and deep trouble. Unemployment, so many problems. Sad, tragic," he sighed. "No, Father, it's not because you control things, but because we all work at being a family. Because we care, love one another. And, the Lord has been good to us," he added softly.

Joseph agreed. "We don't always take time to show our love as openly as we could or should. We could be lots more affectionate, more loving."

He laughed. "These days, it's perfectly okay for men to be tender and loving. Not just women. When we express our love openly and honestly, it makes you feel so good inside."

Keoni sat very still. The open, frank things being said by his brothers surprised him. He had felt those same things so many times but didn't know how to express them.

His voice croaked, hardly more than a whisper as he said, "The first time I ever saw you kiss or hug Mother was the morning I learned about Jeremiah's accident." He looked into Father's eyes. Because Father said nothing, he went on. "I thought it was beautiful. You comforted her in a special way."

He added, "The Talamoa family all seem so

close. They hug and kiss all the time. They are warm, open and loving."

Joseph laughed. "I remember when Papa Talamoa use to crack heads often. I suppose that's a way of being close and expressing feelings, too.."

Mother added, "Hugging and kissing a lot are not the only forms of expressing love and affection."

"It's nice, though," Keoni said, thinking of Soa.

Mother stood up and walked over to where Keoni sat. She hugged him and kissed the top of his head. He turned red.

"It is nice," Mother said, kissing each one of them in turn. "I'm glad you have not gotten too big to kiss or hug. I'm sorry I haven't done it more often." She went to the kitchen and returned with the pot of hot chocolate. She refilled their cups.

Jeremiah sipped his. "You know what, brothers? I think we're all getting older, growing up. Maybe now, Father can and will begin to relax more. Enjoy us in a less stern way."

Father grinned. "You have a point there, Jeremiah. Keoni hasn't totaled the car or wiped himself out on a wave."

"Yet," Keoni laughed.

Father went on. "You survived your accident," he looked at Jeremiah. "As I said at Thanksgiving, we truly have much to be grateful for. I meant those words."

Mother smiled. "Your father is a stern, hard man with all of us. But it's because he loves us. It's not easy for him to express that deep and caring love. That's not the way he was brought up. His nature is different from many of our island people here. It's true, they often show their feelings more openly."

She went on. "But that does not mean your Father doesn't care. He does. You must believe that. I can tell you truthfully, I couldn't have asked for a finer husband or a better father for you boys."

"Every family loves in its own way," Jeremiah said.

"Sometimes, it takes some tough times to learn that. To really come to know it," he winked at Keoni.

"I'm learning," Keoni grinned. "This has been a night of learning for me." He added, "I've been so busy wanting to be somebody else instead of what I am...I think I'm just beginning to come to understand what our family is all about." He laughed. "I like it. I like it."

Father stood up. "We've had a pretty heavy discussion here tonight. I think it's been good for all of us. Family togetherness is important. But," he said, "I think it's time to lighten things up."

He clapped Keoni on the shoulder. "You have plenty of time to learn more about your family. It doesn't all happen in one night. You have so much to learn about people and life. But that's in the future." He laughed, "Right now, I think it's time for you to get out your guitar. Sing for us. Play us some of your surfin' songs."

Joseph, Jeremiah and Mother clapped. "Right on," Joseph said. "You're on, little brother."

Keoni laughed as he went to get his guitar. He felt happy inside. He decided his own family was pretty special. I guess I'm a lucky guy, he thought.

He decided he might even play some church hymns tonight. He knew Father would enjoy that and some Christmas carols too.

He might even call Soa when they had finished to see if she could find a place for him in the special Christmas program at PCC. He had told her he wouldn't play because he'd felt angry before and wasn't into Christmas this year.

Now, he felt full of hope and the spirit of the season. He could hardly wait for Micah to get home to have him share in this special time with the family, too. Keoni grinned, grabbed his guitar and hurried back into the living room to play for his family.

PAU

Other chapter book favorites from
The Adventures in Hawaii Series

Makoa and The Place of Refuge
Written by Jerry Cunnyngham
Illustrated by Sharon Alshams

Makoa is running for his life!... This tale of old Hawaii is about a young boy, Makoa, who has broken a great *kapu* which condemns him to death. Can he reach *Pu'uhonua o Honaunau* (the Place of Refuge) before his pursuers put a spear through his heart?

The Microchip Caper
Written by Robert Graham
Illustrated by Sharon Alshams

Julie and Todd have sailed with their parents and their pet parrot from California to Hawaii. In Honolulu, they became friends with Moana and Kai. The new friends are soon creeping onto a strange boat in the middle of the night as they try to solve the mystery of *The Microchip Caper*.

The Thief in Chinatown
Written by Elaine Masters
Illustrated by Sharon Alshams

There is big trouble in Honolulu's Chinatown in 1896! Six oranges have been stolen from Wong's Grocery. The thief turns out to be a runaway boy from a ship in the harbor. Excitement builds as the Wong family tries to hide and protect the boy who stole their oranges.